M000025649

PHOENIX

FERAL KENYON

Copyright

Phoenix: a poetry book

Feral Kenyon

© 2019, KDP Publishing

Self publishing

feralblacksheep@gmail.com

ALL RIGHTS RESERVED. This book contains material protected under International and Federal Copyright Laws and Treaties. Any unauthorized reprint or use of this material is prohibited. No part of this book may be reproduced or transmitted in any form or by any means, electronic or mechanical, including photocopying, recording, or by any information storage and retrieval system without express written permission from the author / publisher

to brittney and kim

FERAL KENYON

TABLE OF CONTENTS

i. birth of fire

In Mother's belly, of the soil and seed

    I incubate, and feed from the richness of the land,

    the purity and essence of its creatures.

She bellows and screams as she gives birth to fire

      her amniotic fluid staining the hills, the trees, the rivers and lakes.

    the tears of angels and flame mold my body like clay

     and from the ashes, form carnations.

        I become.

FERAL KENYON

I was made from pink and white carnations
grown from the ashes of burned gods
and flourished under the givers of flame

FERAL KENYON

I have known since birth that I was not meant to be small.
my bones ached and protruded from my skin as others attempted
to fit my form into a boxed cage. my eyes burned with the salt of
my tears, but they kept finding new corners to fill. new ways to
distort me until I was within their ideal image. but little did they
know that as my body was twisted and crushed, I became fluid.
like water. I flowed through the cracks and formed something bigger.
harder. meaner. better.
me.

hell was created with me in mind

in my years on this planet, I have
  felt I was not of this earth
and at times, felt sad in my lonesome.
   was there no other
    that felt they were trapped in their own skin?
  none that felt the prison of flesh
   contained a being meant to fly?

FERAL KENYON

I was never meant to be normal.

The circumstances of which I was born made it so. I never knew why the stares that followed me were so cold. Never knew why the warmth that surrounded me did not extend to those in close proximity, but instead burned them when they tried to touch. I didn't see the fire that surrounded my soul to be harmful. It comforted me. Everyone else can adjust.

To be regular meant to be alight for mere seconds
   quick and forgetful,
 before dying as the embers do

   I dread the day I become as such.

sometimes,
  without permission, i should add,
my eyes see the world through a lens
  of which everything is black
and the only thing that makes sense
    is the light inside of me

      - but sometimes that light runs out of energy

it took me so long
to fall in love with
the fire in my soul

as years go by, I gather more of the sun in myself
  not only do I belong to the sun
  and am her passion reincarnate,
  but her radiance belongs to me

it shows in the fiery tongue I was born with --
  spitting fire at anyone that attempts to put out my flame
it shows in the way my skin glows --
  blinding those that would see me in a dim light
it shows in the temper I was bestowed --
  so sharp and hot that even I'm scolded by its burn sometimes

it doesn't bother me
  for even when the winter comes,
    as it often does,
  the frost will not bother me
I will outshine it

I hear they call you the light bringer.

ii. the fall

I will never forget the first time
I laid eyes on a one-winged angel.

I couldn't place why he was so familiar --
    why, even with my stone walls and
    impenetrable skin,
    he was able to find the weakest link
in the chains I'd wrapped around myself
    and break it with a snap of his fingers

he hugged me
and his flesh did not sear
i feel safe

FERAL KENYON

the first time you called me your sunshine
an overwhelming warmness filled me and
i finally knew what it was like to love

instead of running from my fire,
you pulled up your favorite chair
opened your favorite book
and cozied up to the warmness of me.

we lay in the light of the universe
  creating our own galaxies and constellations
    you count the freckles on my face and name them
  as one does stars
 and tell me, with every imperfect spot
reasons you were falling for me.
 when you ask me to be yours
  i don't hesitate

FERAL KENYON

when i have to describe what you mean to me
  i lose all sense of time, space, and words

how does one describe the fire in my belly
  that threatens to consume me when you smile at me?
how does one perfectly capture the authority
  in which you present yourself at your most confident?
how can i possibly tell someone, in the perfect words,
  that if God were to tell me i would be damned if i loved him
  i would spit in His face and tell him to watch me?

FERAL KENYON

the greatest trick the devil ever did
  was convince the world he does not exist
 and yet i see him in you everyday

i see him in the way your charms have evaded and even challenged the
roughest parts of myself
i see him in the sly way you smile when i've said something you find of
interest
i see him in the smoke of the cigarette you've lit out of, seemingly, thin air
i see him in your eyes when they trace the swell of my waist and my
breasts
i see him in the excited way you push your foot to the pedal in the old
impala as the music gets louder and louder

so tell me
  do you have any other tricks?

when i climbed into your lap and pressed my lips to yours
i felt a fire in my heart that i'd only felt in my lonesome
could it be that i found that same flame in you?
were we born of the same fruits of the
tree that sculpted me?

the warmth of my core says yes. we are one.

falling in love with you
   wasn't like how they described in the movies

what was it about you that made me want more? maybe it was the crookedness of your smile that caught my eye when you greeted me. maybe it was the way your midnight hair fell in tresses over your face, and how soft it looked when you brushed it behind your ear. maybe it was the perfect bow-shaped lips that hugged a dozen cigarettes before we were to part at every rendezvous.

no, it had to be your eyes.

those damn eyes that could bring me down to my knees faster than i could have time to pray for mercy. the eyes that held a fire only i'd known from birth. it was those eyes that held the entrance of Hell itself and gave me a glimpse into what lie in wait for me if i fell into them. the eyes that held a gaze so seductively menacing, that if i stared too long i would get drawn in by the obscurity of the act without a hope of ever resurfacing.

those eyes of yours that cursed me.

your silver tongue traces my skin and
   savors every curve you find
with every kiss with every brush with every nip
 it brings forth every beast that lay dormant
   and breaks down every wall i'd built
      stone by stone, brick by brick

the wing on his back
　black as night, unfurling and coming undone
wraps around me,
　　pulling me closer than i thought possible as
　he pushes himself inside of me

i'm praying to a god
i do not believe in, praying he never stop
　his life's work of damning me
and as we scream out our pure relief and bliss
i know he's sealed my fate
　　　　i'd have it no other way

"Please don't leave me."
The sun-kissed complexion I'd grown to love gives way to a moonshine glow. I can count the spider veins in your hands and arms, and they darken the longer I stare. I'm too terrified to move, but I know you're still you.

"I'm still the person you love."
The velvet chocolate of your eyes is burnt beyond what I recognize. They aren't the eyes that took glances when I wasn't looking. They aren't the eyes that told the world of a thousand stories you could never speak out loud, but I learned to read anyway. The endless blackness is so full of despair that I struggle to find the warmth that made me feel safe.

"Please don't think me a monster."
The hair that I would card my hands through to soothe you as you slept is a matted mess, and is longer than what I remember. The mouth that kissed me everyday and whispered sweet nothings is wide enough to swallow me whole. The fear inside of me is endless.

"This is who I really am."

"I'll say this now, and I'll say it for the rest of my life. You are, and will always be, the reason I live." I cradle your head against me and all I can think about is protecting you.

"You're the reason I wake up every morning. You're the reason I go to sleep with a smile on my face. You're the reason I'm alive and never gave up on myself so long ago. You're the reason I love as hard as I do. I found you in this life, and I'll find you in the next. You're mine in any shape or form. And only mine. That will never change as long as I'm breathing the same air as you, and even beyond."

You lift your head from to stare at me, and I don't think you realize how deeply my love for you runs.

"You're amazing," you whisper, and your fingers reach to gently cup my cheek as you nudge your forehead against mine. "Your love is amazing." Even now, holding a broken and fallen angel in my arms, I love you. The sheer depth of my love has no ending. "I will find you in every lifetime, my love. Every lifetime, until there is no time left. And even then, I will always find a way to be with you."

"forever?"

"and always"

FERAL KENYON

FERAL KENYON

what fools we were to promise such things

iii. spiral

the first time we fought
  we were both caught off guard

we spent days dancing around each other
  tip-toeing, ducking, and playing gymnastics
with our words

without any warning, the toeing became stomping
and the hurt became anger

it wasn't something that should have happened
  it had nothing to do with us,
yet there we were

shouting. angry. upset
we weren't us.
that's what i keep telling myself

we weren't us.

"Baby?"
"Yeah?"
"I hate that we fought. We shouldn't have done that."
"I know. I hate that we parted like that."
"Please come home."
"Okay."
"I love you."
"I love you, too."

FERAL KENYON

you kept me in the dark so i couldn't see what you were becoming. so i couldn't see the silver blade hidden on your tongue so that when you kissed me, i felt a sharpness i couldn't place.

i'm bleeding…

i. i asked you to paint a portrait of me with those hands i love --
the ones that strum strings as easy as breathing. the ones that used to
comfort me and cradle my own when in need. the ones i haven't felt on
my body in quite some time. you shed your clothes and take the blade at
your side, slit yourself from nose to navel and the blackness that spills
from you is one i've seen before. but i lay still. it's time for my portrait.
from your ribcage, you break off a branch, a bone-crushing snap that
startles me. "from my bone, shall be the handle of the brush i paint my
love in."

ii. next to you is the jeweled goblet i'd gifted you, intricate and
golden in all its glory, not yet used. meant to be for wine as red as His.
you raise it to me -- a toast to the glory of our sunlit forever -- before you
place it upon your chest and let that liquid blackness fill it to the brim.
"from my blood, shall be the paint of which i paint my love in."

iii. you stand and make your way towards me, almost menacingly
so. you're now standing above me. tall. dark. towering. spilling onto me
your inner darkness. you lift your blade. it's coming towards me. before i
can scream, it comes down only to cut a lock of my long tresses. you lean
forward to kiss me and i'm too frozen to react. why am i so cold? "from
your hair, shall be the ferrule so that i may paint my love. and from my
own, shall be the brush."

iv. you fashion the brush of bone, hair, and blood into your liking, the tar-like substance that covers my skin dripping into the crevasses of my body as if they were fingers gripping me. i can't breathe, but you don't seem to notice. you dip your brush into the black and begin your piece. do you notice the pool of your insides around your feet?

v. i'm choking. the tar has moved from my body to my mouth and i'm struggling to swallow it all. the mucus-like texture crawls against my throat and my insides feel like popping candy. i can't even call out for help while you keep on painting. a flick of the wrist here, a change of direction there, and that smile widens. he's back inside of you.

vi. i try to convince myself it's honey. the tar fills me from the inside out and it's too late. you put the brush down and look down at me. there is no light in the depths of which i'm lost when i stare into your eyes. you turn the painting around and to my horror is me, distorted, disfigured, and disturbing, dressed in the blackness and with eyes that reflected your own. "this, sunshine, is the love i have painted for you."

Will you lick the blood from my hands as i tear myself to pieces?

that chip on your shoulder looks a lot like
where i last laid my lips.

how am i to feel warmth again
when as i dismantle my walls, bare my naked form,
and offer you my very light,
you build from me, shape my skin to leather and
use my bones as cement to keep yourself warm?

"I need some space."
"Okay...is there anything I can do to help?"
"No, not this time."
"Okay. Take all the time you need. I love you."
"......"

FERAL KENYON

FERAL KENYON

"Baby, please tell me you love me."
"You know I do."

i feel insecure. i feel weak.

"I need to hear it from you. Please."
"I love you. I'll see you later."

"Please don't leave me."
my skin is no longer glowing, as the flame inside of me is dimming. i can no longer guide you out of the darkness, and thus i am useless. i am now dull and pale, such a difference in the girl you fell in love with.

"I'm still the person you love."
my eyes are sad. there is a darkness in me that i am begging to get out of, if you'd only reach out to find me. why can't you see me? why is it so dark?

"Please don't think me a monster."
i am but a shell of who i was, and yet i am still full of love. i reach out for you in this darkness and with your night eyes, you divert me every time i try to get closer to you. it's not that you can't see me. you don't want to.

i gave you everything
that must be why
i have
nothing.

you allowed your stresses to warp
how i was treated.
i was drowning in my own blood
and you berated me for getting your floor dirty
when you were the one that put the knife in my back.

i swallowed the hurt and pain
 so you wouldn't see it

maybe i should have spoken.

Please leave a message at the tone.
Please leave a message at the tone.
Please leave a message at the tone.
Please leave a message at the tone.
Please leave a message at the tone.
Please leave a message at the tone.
Please leave a message at the tone.
Please leave a message at the tone.
Please leave a message at the tone.
Please leave a message at the tone.
Please leave a message at the tone.
Please leave a message at the tone.
Please leave a message at the tone.
Please leave a message at the tone.

FERAL KENYON

49 minutes ago

Olivia
[TXT]: Please pick up the phone. I need you.

3 minutes ago

Yuu [TXT]: You have to find someone else.

hear no evil see no evil speak no evil hear no evil see no evil speak no
evil hear no evil see no evil speak no evil hear no evil see no evil speak
no evil hear no evil see no evil speak no evil hear no evil see no evil
speak no evil hear no evil see no evil speak no evil hear no evil see no
evil speak no evil hear no evil see no evil speak no evil hear no evil see
no evil speak no evil hear no evil see no evil speak no evil hear no evil
see no evil speak no evil hear no evil see no evil speak no evil hear no
evil see no evil speak no evil hear no evil see no evil speak no evil hear
no evil see no evil speak no evil hear no evil see no evil speak no evil
hear no evil see no evil speak no evil hear no evil see no evil speak no
evil hear no evil see no evil speak no evil hear no evil see no evil speak
no evil hear no evil see no evil speak no evil hear no evil see no evil
speak no evil hear no evil see no evil speak no evil hear no evil see no
evil speak no evil hear no evil see no evil speak no evil hear no evil see
no evil speak no evil hear no evil see no evil speak no evil hear no evil
see no evil speak no evil hear no evil see no evil speak no evil hear no
evil see no evil speak no evil hear no evil see no evil speak no evil

70

all men do is take
and take
and take
and take
and take
until there's nothing
but bones

FERAL KENYON

you made me carry the weight of the guilt you harbored
because you couldn't stand to confront what you were doing to me

FERAL KENYON

i remember a time
  when i was your sunshine -- a time before you took my warmth
                        and you decided you were no
                        longer mine

i've learned to never trust the promises
  of a sunlit forever
  because forever only takes a second to sever

FERAL KENYON

i am rage and fire and confusion and mourning and agony and hurt and
nothing.
nothing nothing nothing nothing nothing nothing nothing NOTHING.
please make it stop
stop checking on me. stop coming here. stop watching me. if you see this,
please just speak to me instead of watching. i hate the silence. there's been
so much silence. so quiet. there's been so much hurt and I can't even tell
the person that means the most to me how much i'm hurting. because.
i'm not worth the fight anymore. i give and give and give and give until
there's nothing left. there's nothing left of me to give you. i have nothing
anymore. you took it all away. just go or stay. no in between. put me out
of my misery. kill me. please. anything is better than the cold. the quiet.
the ringing in my ears. i'm so fucking sorry for everything. i don't know
what to do anymore. you broke me.
.
go go go go go go GO GO GO GO GO FUCKING G–

FERAL KENYON

She is dead
Just as the ego she had possessed
As the love she was fond of
And the heart that grew too big

All was gone
and in her place
was born a wild woman
reborn

iv. rebirth

here, in this empty house
  that we built with our own two hands
  every nook and cranny filled with memories of us
i stand alone

i'm on my seventh shot of whiskey
  and the drunkenness still doesn't take the pain away
  doesn't take away the ache once i remember
      you chose to leave for a reason i was never told

i feel my stomach in my throat and it's not long
    before i'm purging all that is inside me
  the honey you fed me tastes like cigarettes and rot
  the blackness pooling around my feet

i rid myself of you

i'm afraid to keep going
  because i know once i say goodbye
  there's no turning back

I was robbed of choice and of my closure.
and so I must drink my whiskey
grind my teeth
and sew the stitches of my heart together
with my own hand

you may have taken my warmth
and left me to freeze
but what you didn't know was that
I am a phoenix. and from my ashes
will birth a new woman
that will never have been touched by you

The straight jacket I've tied
around me is custom made in
barbed wire, teeth, and…
the last words you said to me.

-     but I'll be okay.

FERAL KENYON

she doesn't want your sorries
　　or your pretty goodbyes
she doesn't want your beautiful lies
　　that made her cry
begging for another way would be ideal
but then again
　　what else could she try?

learning to be without you
  was like swallowing hot glass
        ripping open a nail bed
        or going without your regular fix
it was like walking on shards of ice
  in the middle of an Alaskan blizzard
  and hoping a warm blanket was on the other side

and though my journey was difficult, I survived
  maybe we didn't get to rule the world
  maybe our forever was cut short
  maybe we weren't meant to be

but I thank you for showing me how to love anyway.
I wouldn't have changed a thing.

I was angry for a long time. I still am, if I think about it too hard. You were the person I thought would be in my life forever, but now you'll have to be a distant memory. Every time I love someone, there will be an echo of you in them. I wonder if all of the sleepless nights where I cried til the sun rose will ever be worth how much time I spent doing it.

if one were to take my heart from my chest
   and put it on display for all to see
      they would find your name in the form
of scar tissue
         but I will be healed.

I know you were in pain, too.
I hope you heal.
I hope you've learned.
I hope that the next person you meet will
see in you what I saw and love you harder.
I hope you have the courage to stay.
and though I'll be jealous of your peace without me,
know that I love you so much
and I couldn't grow without the lessons you taught me.

FERAL KENYON

It's true – I am damaged
  I am bent and worn, and
  dirtied, tattered, and torn
however that may be, I am unbroken.
in all my wars both inside and out
  I remain the victor – and the
scar tissue that surrounds
  my soul will forever be
      impenetrable

I will always love you.
I just respect myself enough
to know I deserve better.
I deserve someone that will face
our fears alongside me
instead of running away to stay safe

You may never have intended to hurt me, but don't you dare paint me as the villain when you were the rail I held during every step towards my descent to madness.

FERAL KENYON

I needed you to let me kill myself. to overdose on the last of that awesome fix you filled me with for exactly one thousand eight hundred and forty-six days.

I needed you to let me go through the withdrawals – the aches and pains of needing you. of you being
within reach. of almost – but not quite – being sober and free to think. nothing will ever quite explain
        the shakes, the anxiety, the pain
        of you.

I needed to be in so much pain that everyone within reach felt my talons dig at their skin, felt me bathing in their blood and tears as they resuscitate me and try to squeeze your poisonous promises from my veins.

I needed you to watch me suffer and do nothing so I could learn how to stand up for myself again. I needed you to believe the lies you told yourself so I could learn how to confess my own wrongdoings but take no blame for your own shitty actions.

I needed you to let me burn in the flames of the fire that was set inside of me and burned me from the inside out so that I may rise as something you'll have never touched. I needed you to let me kill myself so that I could be reborn from the ashes of my own scorched self.

I needed you.

I needed you to do everything you did
so I can finally say

goodbye

now watch me rise.

FERAL KENYON

Feral Kenyon is an Atlanta-born writer, musician, and photographer. As a child, she was always drawn to the darker side of human nature, and as she grew up that curiosity grew with her. Even though she'd written many short stories and poems growing up, the roleplay community on Tumblr was the gateway into her writing seriously. Though she dropped out of college to pursue a different path, she still enjoys studying religion, music, and photography. She currently resides in south Atlanta with her two cats and a cup of boba within arms reach at all times.

You can find her on Instagram at @feralblacksheep

FERAL KENYON

Made in the USA
Las Vegas, NV
02 May 2022

48338812R00059